ariel and emily

Adele Aron Greenspun and Joanie Schwarz

DUTTON CHILDREN'S BOOKS • NEW YORK

Copyright © 2003 by Adele Aron Greenspun

Library of Congress Cataloging-in-Publication Data
Greenspun, Adele Aron.
Ariel and Emily/by Adele Aron Greenspun and Joanie Schwarz.—1st ed.
p. cm.
Summary: Two young girls who are best friends have fun playing together at the park.
ISBN 0-525-46861-7
[1. Best Friends—Fiction. 2. Friendship—Fiction. 3. Parks—Fiction.] I. Schwarz, Joanie.
II. Title.
PZ7.G85195 Ar 2003 [E]—dc21 2001040399

Published in the United States 2003 by Dutton Children's Books,
a division of Penguin Putnam Books for Young Readers
345 Hudson Street, New York, New York 10014
www.penguinputnam.com

Designed by Alyssa Morris and Irene Vandervoort

Printed in Hong Kong
First Edition
10 9 8 7 6 5 4 3 2 1

For Ariel and Emily, Lee, Dean, Frances, and Bert, with love
A.A.G.

To Lee and Dean, with love
J.S.

This is Ariel.

This is Emily.

Best friends.

Ariel and Emily love to go to the park.

The park is full of surprises.

It's the perfect place to be silly . . .

. . . and make a lot of noise!

Sometimes Ariel and Emily

play by themselves.

But mostly they play together.

Ariel builds with blocks . . .

and Emily helps her crash them.

Emily blows bubbles . . .

and Ariel helps her pop them.

They share a squishy banana snack.

Then it's time for hide-and-seek.

Where's Emily?

There she is !

That's the fun of hide-and-seek . . .

. . . finding each other again.

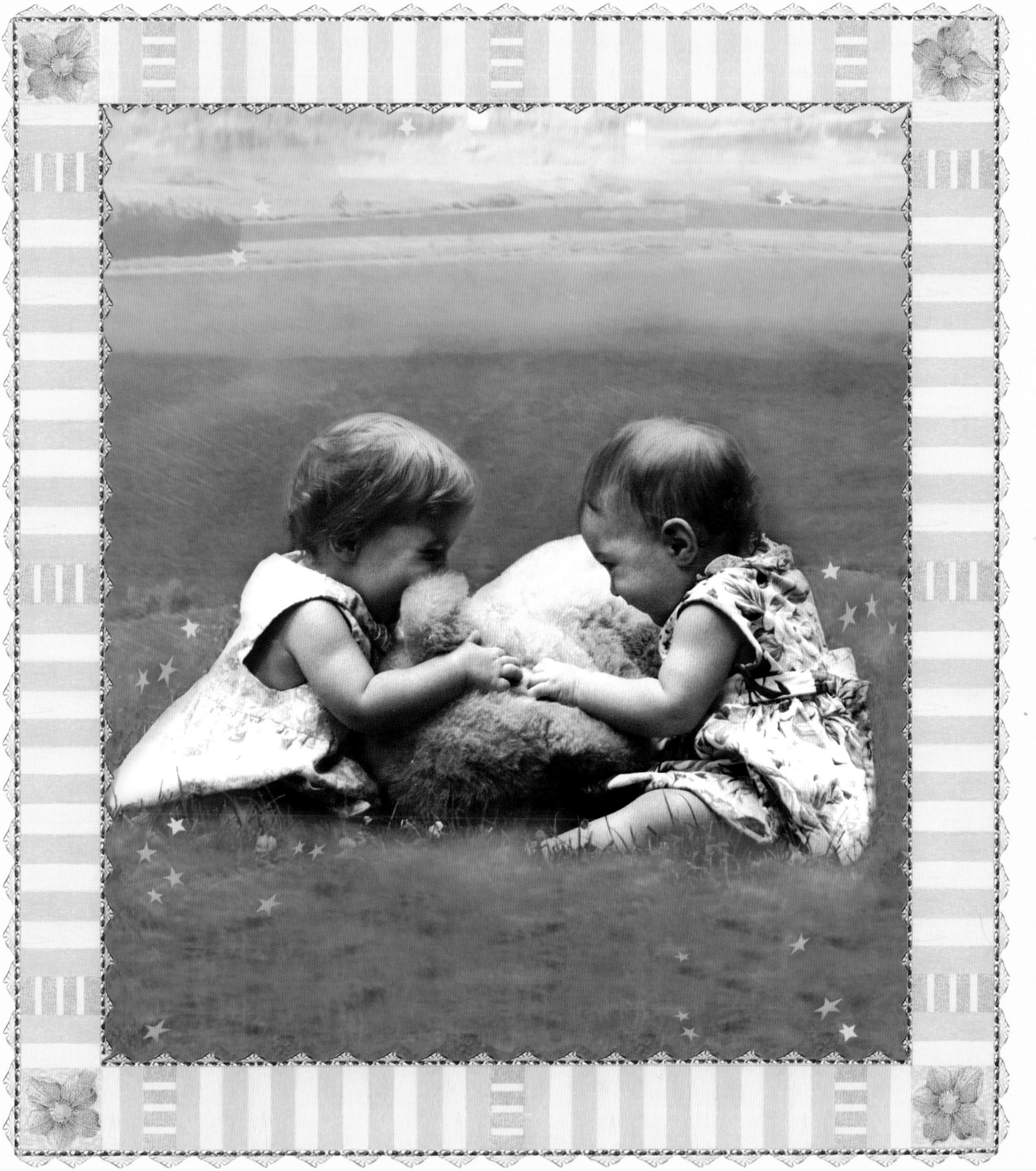

Ariel and Emily. Best friends.